JEREMY B[image_ref]
THE MUM[...]

CW00864564

Imagine if one of your classmates was really a secret agent like James Bond! Well, Jeremy Brown is – and this is the second story about his funny, action-packed adventures!

Simon Cheshire has written stories since he was at school, but it was only after turning thirty that he realized "my mental age would never exceed ten and that, in children's books, I had finally found my natural habitat". He has written three stories about Jeremy Brown – *Jeremy Brown of the Secret Service* (his first published book), *Jeremy Brown and the Mummy's Curse* and *Jeremy Brown on Mars*. The stories, he claims, "are based entirely upon actual events. Only names, characters, plots, dialogue and descriptive content have been changed, to make them more believable." He is also the author of *They Melted His Brain!*, *Totally Unsuitable for Children* and *Dirty Rotten Tricks*.

Books by the same author

Jeremy Brown of the Secret Service
Jeremy Brown on Mars

For older readers

Dirty Rotten Tricks
They Melted His Brain!
Totally Unsuitable for Children

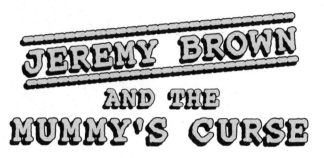

JEREMY BROWN
AND THE
MUMMY'S CURSE

SIMON CHESHIRE

Illustrations by
HUNT EMERSON

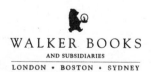

WALKER BOOKS
AND SUBSIDIARIES
LONDON • BOSTON • SYDNEY

To George with love

First published 1998 by Walker Books Ltd
87 Vauxhall Walk, London SE11 5HJ

This edition published 2000

2 4 6 8 10 9 7 5 3 1

Text © 1998 Simon Cheshire
Illustrations © 1998 Hunt Emerson

The right of Simon Cheshire to be identified as author
of this work has been asserted by him in accordance with the
Copyright, Designs and Patents Act 1988.

This book has been typeset in Plantin.

Printed and bound in Great Britain
by The Guernsey Press Co. Ltd

British Library Cataloguing in Publication Data
A catalogue record for this book
is available from the British Library.

ISBN 0-7445-7801-9

Contents

Chapter 1

In which Jeremy Brown shakes with fear and a mummy comes to life

....

Jeremy Brown's secret was safe. Everyone at Grotside School thought of him as that weedy kid with the glasses. Only his best friend Patsy Spudd knew that underneath the clever disguise, he was an MI7 agent. And a rather brilliant one at that, he always thought.

Of course, if he'd paid the same attention to his schoolwork as he did to catching crooks and saving the world, he'd have already got twelve A-levels, and a degree from the University of Brains. As it was, he came bottom in everything, unless Patsy beat him to it.

It was Friday afternoon, double Maths with Mr Algebra, and everyone was fed up.

"I'm fed up," mumbled Patsy, too fed up to

say anything more original. She kept curling her ginger hair around her fingers.

Mr Algebra wrote a set of formulas on the blackboard. If Jeremy had been paying attention, he'd have realized that they were perfect for helping to decode electronic locking systems. But he wasn't. Instead, he was thinking about his last mission, and how very clever he'd been in proving that diamonds were being smuggled out of the country by a little old lady from Swanage.

"Who'd have thought it," said Jeremy. "Hollow teeth."

"It was me who extracted them," said Patsy. "She might have been ninety-seven, but she still kicked like a mule," she added, rubbing her left leg.

The class stared vacantly at the blackboard with droopy eyes and ever droopier mouths. Some of them were bored to tears (and were wringing out their hankies), some of them were bored stupid (and had forgotten their names), but luckily none of them had been bored to death yet.

"I wish MI7 would call me with a case," muttered Jeremy. Very soon, he'd be wishing he hadn't said that. And to find out why, we must first go to Cairo…

The museum was dark, silent and smelt of old socks. It was the smell of thousands of years of ancient Egyptian history. Mummy cases lined the walls, and huge stone statues of gods and animals stood in every corner.

The last visitor of the day had left hours ago. Agent Spanner of MI7 wandered along the upper gallery of the main hall, keeping a sharp eye out for something he knew was there, somewhere. His footsteps echoed around the walls. He was wearing a smart white suit, which is probably the silliest thing you can wear in a hot, sticky climate like Egypt's, but he'd seen people wear them in films on the telly, so he reckoned he looked cool.

He dabbed the sweat off his forehead with his sleeve. It left a grubby stain. At last, he stopped in front of a particularly large, coffin-like and frightening-looking wooden sarcophagus. It was covered in ancient Egyptian hieroglyphics, and a large, noble face was painted near its top in black and gold. Agent Spanner gulped quietly. "The casket of Psidesalad II," he whispered.

With both hands gripping one edge of the lid, he heaved the mummy case open. It creaked and groaned. A scattering of dust puffed up and settled nervously around his feet, glad to be out of there.

The mummy, its arms folded across its chest, stood tall and terrifying before him. It was wrapped tightly in bandages, and the bandages were wrapped tightly in dirt.

"Eurgh, it's a bit mucky," he mumbled to himself.

A thin beam of blue light ran from one side of the case to the other, level with the mummy's knees. Carefully, Agent Spanner reached out and broke the beam with his fingers.

His scream of fright was, just at that moment, the loudest noise in Cairo. The mummy's tightly encased hands had jerked into life. With sudden, sharp movements it grabbed the sides of the case and hauled itself forward.

Agent Spanner jumped back. The mummy's feet landed with twin thuds on the stone floor. He jumped back some more. The mummy stood up straight, towering over him. Agent Spanner would have liked to jump back roughly as far as France, but he was now pressed tightly against an exhibit of primitive farming tools.

The mummy closed in. Agent Spanner's eyes bulged out of his face like golf balls sitting on a pizza...

Jeremy's eyes were also bulging. He'd fixed his lids open with sticky tape in an effort to look alert, but all it was doing was making his eyes water.

"Did I tell you about when I had to glue

my knees together to prop a bank vault door open?"

"Many times," sighed Patsy.

Suddenly, Jeremy's tie began to make a tiny beeping noise. He sat up straight, wide awake. The rest of the class turned to peer sleepily at him. Mr Algebra craned his neck and shuffled from side to side. "Brown? Are you emitting a peculiar noise?"

Jeremy thought quickly. "Er, yes sir. It's my lower intestine. Very embarrassing personal problem, sir. Could erupt any minute."

Mr Algebra shuffled in horror at the thought of his lovely classroom awash with… "Quick! Get out! Find the school nurse! Or a toilet!"

"Thank you, sir," said Jeremy. All but one member of the class giggled cruelly as he dashed for the door. The odd one out was, of course, Patsy. She knew very well what that beeping meant.

Outside, in the chalky corridor, Jeremy quickly checked that nobody could see him.

He stuck one end of his tie into his ear (the end with the miniature speaker in it) and held the other close to his mouth (the end with the miniature microphone).

"The fairy cakes are made of sponge," said the deep voice of his boss at MI7.

"With big red cherries on the top," responded Jeremy correctly. "Morning, boss."

"Good morning, Agent Brown. Pay attention. A week ago, we lost contact with one of our overseas operatives, Agent Wrench. He'd been sent to Egypt, to guard an exhibition of relics on loan from the British Museum. After several days of silence, we sent a second operative, Agent Spanner, to track him down. Spanner discovered local reports of an ancient curse, which Agent Wrench had apparently fallen victim to."

Jeremy was starting to get a sinking feeling. "And what happened then?"

"No idea. Spanner vanished too. Swallowed up by the curse of the pharaoh

Psidesalad II, by all accounts."

"Oh." It was at this point that Jeremy began shaking with fear, as mentioned at the start of the chapter.

"Your mission," continued the boss, "is to go to Egypt, find out what's going on and stop it."

"I see… Er, wouldn't this be better tackled by … someone … a bit … taller, maybe?"

"Sorry, Brown. Every other agent is off on a training exercise – How to Confuse Your Enemies With a Garden Hose. You're the only one left. Operation Exit will be launched, as normal."

Jeremy's secret radio beeped, spluttered and switched off. Moments later, the bell for the end of the lesson shattered the silence, not to mention his nerves. His legs wobbled and gave way of their own accord. As he got up off the floor and tried to look dignified, Patsy appeared at his side.

"I take it we're off?" she said eagerly.

His everyday disguise was redundant once

more. Time for Jeremy to stop looking weedy and scruffy and start looking all heroic and smart. He straightened his tie, pulled up his socks and put on his special eagle-eyed look. Then he gave Patsy a quick summary of the situation. "MI7 chose me specially," he said. "The others all wanted the job, but there's only me brilliant enough to tackle it, of course."

"We're off, then!" grinned Patsy.

Operation Exit, meanwhile, involved MI7 telephoning the Headmaster of Grotside School. He was told that he should sign a letter allowing both of them to be out of lessons for as long as they wanted, otherwise the world would get to hear about his visits to the Peter Pixie Dressing-Up Club.

Jeremy and Patsy collected their letter from his trembling hands on the way out of the school gates and hurried to the airport. They flew to Cairo in the time it takes to start a new chapter.

Chapter 2

In which Jeremy, Patsy and a camel are shot at with poison darts

··

It was hot. Very, very hot. Think of the wave of heat you get when the oven door is opened. It was hotter than that.

"Oooh, it's hot," said Jeremy. He and Patsy had taken a taxi from Cairo Airport, but after the taxi driver had made them give it back, they'd caught the bus. They had now arrived at a busy, dusty, noisy and quite amazingly hot bus station outside the famous Museum of Antiquities.

Patsy had remembered to bring her wide-brimmed sunhat, and had it jammed tightly on her head, but Jeremy had to keep squinting. A short, round man wearing trendy sunglasses and what looked like an enormous nightshirt came bustling out of the museum and shook their hands warmly.

Patsy was going to make a joke about pyjamas, but didn't. "It's not a nightshirt, it's called a gallibiyya," whispered Jeremy. "Traditional Arab dress."

"Sheik Yabelli," said the round man, with a broad grin. Jeremy and Patsy looked at each other for a moment, then realized that this was his name. "I'm in charge of the British Museum exhibits while they're here in Egypt," he said.

"I am Jeremy Brown of the Secret Service," announced Jeremy in his most official-sounding voice. "And this is my Operations Co-ordinator, Patsy Spudd."

CrunCHH-chomp!

Patsy spun around, ready to thump whoever had just snatched her hat away. She found herself staring up into the face of a dopey-looking camel. The last shreds of her hat were just vanishing between its teeth.

"This is my camel, Deidre," said Sheik Yabelli proudly. "Say hello, Deidre."

Deidre snorted loudly at Patsy. Patsy wiped her face clean, grumbling rudely under her breath.

"I named her Deidre in honour of my favourite aunt," said the Sheik.

"Why, does your aunt like camels?" asked Jeremy.

"No, she just looks like one," said the Sheik. "MI7 informed me you'd be arriving. In view of the fact that the curse of Psidesalad II has already gobbled up two of your agents, I have arranged a bodyguard for you."

Two pairs of piercing, narrow eyes darted into view, behind which lurked the Sheik's henchmen, Mustafa and Dontafa. They, too, wore long, flowing gallibiyyas. Patsy thought they looked like they'd both sell their grannies for half a dozen trading cards and a jam doughnut. Jeremy just thought they were terrifying.

"Hello, boys," he said, with a polite but wobbly smile.

Mustafa and Dontafa bowed low, and said nothing. It was lucky that their bows almost brought their noses to ground level, because otherwise they'd have been hit by the poison darts which now flew over their backs.

Patsy kicked Jeremy hard on the hip, and he was thrown sideways. The darts missed his shoulder by millimetres and embedded themselves into the side of a passing wooden cart.

"Ow!" yelled Jeremy.

"You'd have been oww-ing worse than that if they'd hit you!" said Patsy. "Look!"

As the cart disappeared into the crowds, they could see that the wood around the area where the darts had struck was turning black.

"Poisoned," said Jeremy quietly. "Where did they come from?"

Phhh-eeoooo! Phhh-eeoooo! Two more bounced off the pavement by their feet. Mustafa and Dontafa were suddenly nowhere to be seen. Sheik Yabelli was spinning on the spot, looking this way and that.

Jeremy remembered what he'd read in MI7's "How to Spot Trouble" brochure. He quickly analyzed his surroundings: lots of people, lots of cars and three really enormous camels. Much bigger than Deidre. And sort of ... shiny-looking!

The head of one of the big camels suddenly swivelled round. Its perfectly round eyes zoomed in on him. Where there should have been pupils, there were cross hairs, like the rangefinder of a gun. The camel's head jutted forward. Slots slid open across its nostrils.

Phhh-eeoooo! Phhh-eeoooo! Jeremy dropped to the dusty pavement. The darts whizzed over his head.

"They're after us!" he yelled at Patsy. Now he'd got his shirt all grubby, and that made things even worse as far as he was concerned.

Patsy began to make a dash for it, but there was too much traffic. Every direction was blocked with people, buses, taxis, carts and market stalls!

Phhh-eeoooo! Phhh-eeoooo! Smack into the

front tyre of a bicycle. The rider pitched over into the back of a truck-load of manure, which carried him away with his legs wriggling wildly in the air.

A dart could hit one of the crowd at any moment! Jeremy had an idea.

"Sheik!" he called. "Can we borrow Deidre?"

Sheik Yabelli had taken cover under Ibrahim's Pet Parade stall, behind a sign saying LITTLE BIRDIES, GOING CHEAP. His hand poked out in a quick thumbs-up sign.

The three big camels were marching through the crowd, heads turning, target sensors homing in on Jeremy and Patsy. Their legs whirred and *ka-clunk*ed as they walked.

"Are they what I think they are?" whispered Patsy.

"Yes," said Jeremy. "Robot camels with nasal armaments!"

Patsy jumped up on to Deidre's back and hauled Jeremy up after her. Remembering her camel driving lessons, she tugged on Deidre's ears. "Move!" she bellowed. Deidre lurched and bucked.

The robots instantly turned to pursue them, walking faster.

Deidre, not being the most intelligent animal in the world, bounded ahead in a straight line, and bounding ahead in a straight line meant going right over the roofs of the cars. Jeremy and Patsy hung on as best they could. Deidre crunched her way across one vehicle after another, closely followed by various threats of legal action, and beheading.

The robots increased their speed. They took a different approach with the traffic. They kicked it out of the way. A taxi was hurled over the railings of the museum. The fleeing crowd was splattered with bits of squashed fruit from a shattered cart.

Patsy tugged on Deidre's right ear, and the camel took a sharp turn down a narrow sidestreet lined with shops. The way ahead was more or less clear, and Deidre got up to a full gallop. The sound of cars being crunched was close behind them.

Back in the street, an enormous lorry, carrying rocks, skidded and crushed one of the robots under its wheels. The robot's casing split, showering the street with sparks and circuits. The remaining two ignored it. They turned right, down the sidestreet.

Jeremy took a quick glance back. The robots were galloping too, and much faster than Deidre. They'd catch up in seconds. Their heads jutted forward, and their nostrils whirred open.

"Who's controlling them?" shouted Patsy.

"I could make a couple of guesses!" shouted Jeremy. "But right now I'm more worried about the—"

Phhh-eeoooo! Phhh-eeoooo!

Dozens of darts buzzed through the air. Jeremy and Patsy dodged left and right, gripping tightly on to Deidre's tough, shaggy coat (which was so tough and shaggy that darts simply bounced off it). Deidre galloped as fast as she could, her tongue lolling out. Her wet, slobbery lips flapped in the wind.

Phhh-eeoooo! Phhh-eeoooo! Darts struck the canvas awnings of some of the shops. Shoppers and shopkeepers dived out of the way. The robots moved faster, and faster. Jeremy could smell the engine oil in their joints.

Oil! Something slippery! Jeremy looked up the street, which wasn't easy with Deidre bumping and weaving all over the place. Ahead was a large stall selling shampoo and soap.

"Patsy!" called Jeremy. "Hair gel!"

"Can't you forget your bloomin' hair for once?" cried Patsy. Then she realized what he meant. She gave a sharp nod, held on extra tight around Deidre's neck with her legs and flung herself sideways. As they shot past the stall, she reached out and plucked off a jumbo-sized tub of gel. The weight of it almost dragged her under Deidre's thundering feet. She grunted and struggled, and pulled herself back upright, then quickly handed the tub to Jeremy.

A dart *peee-oww*ed through the shoulder of Jeremy's blazer, turning a little patch of it black. Now he was REALLY cross. Taking aim as accurately as possible (which meant not at all accurately, in the circumstances), he flung the tub of gel.

It spun in a neat arc and burst with a sloppy *splop* on the ground. The robot that was bringing up the rear stepped straight in it. Its legs buckled and slipped. It flipped helplessly head over heels, smacked into a wall and exploded in a deafening clap of thunder and a ball of flame.

The other robot ignored it, and carried on running.

"I bet this sort of thing never happens to the tourists," grumbled Patsy.

*　　*　　*

A group of thirty-two tourists, on a package tour organized by Sun & Sand Holidays Ltd, were at that moment enjoying a leisurely sightseeing cruise down the River Nile. The Sun & Sand representative was speaking to them slowly and calmly:

"So here we are, on the Nile, in the centre of bustling Cairo, the capital of Egypt. On your left, fishing boats, known as feluccas. On your right, busy streets full of shops where you can buy souvenirs and ..." (a puzzled pause) "racing camels?"

The tourists turned, curious. Sure enough a camel, carrying two Europeans, had just shot out from one of the narrow sidestreets.

Up ahead, the end of the street was in sight.

"The river!" shouted Jeremy. "We can short-circuit it!"

Patsy grinned gleefully. She was going to enjoy this bit.

The last robot was right behind them. Darts rained down around Deidre's feet.

*　　*　　*

The tourists watched silently as a real camel, followed by a robot one, leapt at high speed off the tall bank of the Nile. The real camel hit their boat feet-first. The robot tumbled into the water.

The weight of the real camel smashed through the seats, smashed a hole in the boat's bottom, and deposited Jeremy and Patsy on top of the Sun & Sand representative. The boat sank. Mrs Bedsit (from Hull) screamed at the top of her voice. Mr Bungalow (from Leamington Spa) was knocked unconscious by a lump of flying robot.

The water flooded the robot's gears and blew all its circuits. Like the boat, it quickly sank out of sight.

"I think we gave them the hump," said Jeremy.

Deidre doggie-paddled, or rather camel-paddled, to the shore. The tourists demanded their money back.

Chapter 3

In which darkness falls, and so does a sarcophagus

Two hours later, four things had happened.
1.) Deidre had been returned to Sheik
Yabelli, safe and sound. 2.) News of the
camel attack had spread, creating fearful
whispers throughout Cairo about the curse of
Psidesalad II. 3.) The sun had set, and long,
black shadows had crept through the streets,
beneath a sky streaked with a fiery red.
4.) Jeremy had put on a clean shirt.

The Sheik had found Jeremy and Patsy
rooms at the remarkably large and
remarkably shiny Pyramids Palace Hotel.
They checked in wearing dark glasses and
false beards, and using the fake identities of
Mr N. Code and Miss D. Cypher.

"Lucky I'm a master of disguise," said
Jeremy. "Nobody will guess we're undercover
agents now. Whoever sent the robot camels

after us might be searching the hotels, so we must be careful."

They had dinner in the hotel's remarkably posh restaurant, hiding behind their menus. Jeremy had an exotic mix of traditional Eastern dishes – mazzah to start, then kusheri and fattah, followed by baklava. Patsy had pie and chips.

"I can't take you anywhere," grumbled Jeremy.

"I like chips," hissed Patsy through gritted teeth.

With the moon high in the sky, they made their way to the museum. The Sheik had lent them a key. Jeremy wasn't keen on wandering around a dark and mysterious old building in the middle of the night, especially when there were ancient curses lurking about the place. However, Patsy called him a big weedy weed, and he changed his mind.

The huge, wooden front door shut with a clangorous thud behind them. The sound echoed off the massive stone pillars that rose up high into the gloom, then got hopelessly lost among the statues and glass cases. Jeremy switched on the torch they'd also borrowed from the Sheik.

"This place smells of old socks," mumbled Patsy, wrinkling her nose up.

Jeremy examined a small figurine of a jackal-headed god. "Should have paid more attention in History," he said. "Now then, time to bring my simply enormous brainpower into play and find some clues."

Patsy pulled an uh-oh-here-we-go face. Jeremy pretended he hadn't seen.

"Do we have a clear idea of exactly what's going on?" he said.

"No," said Patsy.

"Have we got any firm leads on what might have happened to Agent Wrench and Agent Spanner?"

"No," said Patsy.

"So, we're not doing too badly, so far, are we?"

"No," said Patsy.

A sharp beam of torchlight wobbled ahead of them as they tiptoed around the displays, up a wide stone staircase, along a narrow corridor, through a room filled with manuscripts, past a model of an ancient Egyptian village … and realized they were completely lost. Then they remembered the map that they'd also borrowed from the Sheik, and soon arrived at the tall, vaulted gallery where the mummy cases stood.

Jeremy ran the torch beam up and down each case. They didn't get much of a look at the beautiful designs and skilful carvings on them, because his hand was shaking with fright.

"Oh, give it here," said Patsy, pulling the torch away from him.

"This one over here must be one of the exhibits from London. This is the sarcophagus of Psidesalad II," whispered Patsy.

Jeremy gazed up at it, his eyes nearly as wide open as his mouth. "How do you know?" he breathed. "Can you read the hieroglyphics on the casing?"

"No, I can read the label on the side which says PROPERTY OF THE BRITISH MUSEUM. Shine the torch here, along the floor."

There were footprints and marks in the dust, all over the wooden boards. Hundreds of visitors had passed this spot in the last few days, but Jeremy picked out two sets of prints which came closer to the sarcophagus than all the others.

"Look," he whispered. "One pair of ordinary-sized feet, one pair so big they'd make King Kong wet his pants. The ordinary feet jump backwards, away from the others, as if they're trying to escape." (These were Agent Spanner's footprints, as made on page 12.)

"How do you know they're going backwards?" asked Patsy.

"Because they go right up to this glass

exhibit case, but they're facing away from it. Whoever it was – maybe Agent Wrench or Agent Spanner – clearly didn't walk through the glass case and towards the sarcophagus. The glass case is full and unbroken. So he must have been going backwards from the sarcophagus to the glass case. See?"

Patsy didn't. "You mean he came out of the sarcophagus?" she said, puzzled.

"No, the enormous footprints come out of the sarcophagus," said Jeremy.

They looked at each other for a second. Shivery sensations gleefully played football in their stomachs. Without a sound, Patsy shone the torch along the side of the sarcophagus. There wasn't a trace of dust along its edge.

"Recently opened," gulped Jeremy.

"We'd better take a look inside," said Patsy.

"We'd better call MI7 for back-up. Tanks, cars with sirens, that sort of thing."

"No time," said Patsy. She gripped the edge of the mummy case and heaved it open. It creaked and groaned. The torch lit up the tightly bandaged face of the mummy inside. Its arms were crossed over its chest, and it towered above them.

"Big bloke, wasn't he?" trembled Jeremy.

With a sudden rush of fear to the head, Patsy slammed the lid shut again. As you may have guessed, she was a lass who was stronger than she looked, and the force of the slam made the whole sarcophagus wobble dangerously. Their efforts to stop its rocking motion only managed to make things worse.

"Jump!" yelled Patsy. "It's coming down."

They dodged sideways as the heavy wooden case hit the floor with a shattering crunch. It instantly split into a hundred pieces.

The shattering crunch's echo died away, and the dust began to settle. In the shaky torchlight, they could see the mummy lying face down in the debris. Was that the sound of the broken pieces settling? Or were they being moved aside? Was that the moon throwing eerie shadows across the room? Or was the mummy trying to stand up?

"Oh, crumbs," whispered Jeremy.

It was unmistakable now. With slow, jerky movements, the mummy was clambering to its feet. Pieces of sarcophagus were swept away with casual swats of its chunky, wrapped hands. As it reached its full height, it turned to face them. Its arms reached out for them.

"I think," said Patsy, "that this is the bit where we RUUUUUUNN!"

In their fright, they ran into each other, and various exhibits, as much as they ran for the exit. Not that they knew where the exit was any more – the map was somewhere under all that mess.

The mummy lurched forwards, straight at them. They turned a corner and found themselves in a long room lined with mummy cases. The sound of slow, heavy footsteps thudded in the darkness behind them.

"I've got a brilliant idea," said Jeremy. "But it's revolting, so I won't tell you what it is."

"Hide in the mummy cases!" cried Patsy. "Brilliant!"

"Eurgh!" squirmed Jeremy.

"They're only dead bodies!" said Patsy. "Or would you rather be got by King Tut back there?"

They each chose a sarcophagus, and hauled the lids open. Leaping inside, however, was not an option. Bandaged arms instantly lunged at them. Mummies, every bit as huge as the first one, stepped out. The lids of the other cases in the room slowly creaked open.

Jeremy and Patsy turned and dashed back the way they had come. Then they realized that the first mummy was back that way, so instead they turned and dashed along the gallery which overlooked the main hall.

"This is where commando combat training comes in handy," gasped Jeremy.

"Yes. If only you'd had some," said Patsy.

Fortunately, the stairs down to the hall were straight ahead of them. Unfortunately, up the stairs were coming half a dozen more mummies. Jeremy and Patsy skidded to a halt.

"Trapped!" said Patsy.

Jeremy leaned over the gallery's railings, looking down into the gloom of the hall. They couldn't simply jump over – too high. He ran over to the nearest exhibits – a statue that was far too heavy to move, a mummified cat and an oar from an ancient boat.

The mummies closed in on both sides. The thumping of their enormous feet made the floor shake.

Jeremy grabbed the mummified cat and started to unravel its bandages. He tied one end around the railings.

"I hope this moggie was well fed," he said. "We need enough wrappings to climb down at least thirty metres!"

Patsy quickly wound out the wrappings over the edge, tying loose ends together as she went. She nearly mentioned something about these strips of cloth being two thousand years old and therefore unlikely to take their weight, but she didn't. She soon wished she had.

The mummies emerged from the shadows. They were barely an arm's length away. A mummy's arm's length, that is.

"Move!" yelled Patsy. Clinging on tightly, the two of them launched themselves over the railings, and dropped. Two of the mummies swung their fists, but only succeeded in hitting each other. The one closest to the railings was knocked over them.

Jeremy and Patsy fell for the height of two double-decker buses before the cat's wrappings reached their limit and pulled tight. Sure enough, two-thousand-year-old strips of cloth are complete rubbish when it comes to dangling in mid-air from a railing. They snapped instantly, but the sudden jerk that snapped them was also enough to break Jeremy's and Patsy's fall. They hit the stone floor of the main hall with a variety of painful thuds, but fortunately with no bones broken.

The falling mummy almost landed on top of them, making dents and cracks in the floor. Its innards made a crashing, coming-apart-at-the-seams noise. The bandages around its right arm came loose, revealing shiny metal beneath.

"They're robots too!" said Patsy.

"Thought as much," fibbed Jeremy. "I, er ... never believed all that curse business, anyway."

The other mummies were now lumbering down the stairs. Jeremy and Patsy hurriedly untangled themselves from the heap of wrappings and bits of smashed robot that littered the floor. Without looking back – without looking anywhere, really, because it was especially dark down here – they scrambled for the front door.

The damage they caused by bumping into things and knocking them over was nothing compared to the damage caused by the mummies bumping into things and knocking them over.

With the sound of pounding feet and disintegrating relics ringing in their ears, Jeremy and Patsy flung open the door and ran across the museum gardens. The mummies were still in pursuit, crowding through the door and spreading out to cover the grounds.

Jeremy and Patsy jumped on to the back of a passing horse and cart. Jeremy was relieved to find that it was carrying rolls of cloth, and not something smelly.

"Good evening," he called politely to the sleepy driver. "Could I possibly ask you to drive us away from here very, very fast indeed?"

The driver turned, rubbing his eyes. "Huh?" he grunted. Then he caught sight of the mummies. Pausing only for him to scream, the cart shot away into the night.

Chapter 4

In which Patsy is nearly sick, and Jeremy uses his comb

···

The cup shook, and the tea in the cup shook in time with it, and all because Sheik Yabelli's hand was shaking too. As he held the cup delicately, his little finger poked out at an angle, and that was shaking worst of all.

The Sheik, Jeremy and Patsy were sitting on big fluffy cushions, in a neatly ordered room in the Sheik's house. It was early the next morning. Patsy hadn't yet noticed that Deidre (curled up on a carpet behind her) was nibbling at her hair. Household staff wandered back and forth, doing the laundry, tidying up and listening in on the conversation.

"A most interesting story, Mr Brown," said the Sheik, adjusting his sunglasses. "It appears that our museum, our pride and joy, has been taken over by monsters."

"Robots," corrected Patsy.

"Still monsters in my book," said the Sheik. He took a nervous slurp of tea. Jeremy and Patsy did the same. "And they are beginning to move around throughout the city," he continued. "Nobody will take action against them. Not even the army. The power of the ancient curse is upon us."

"The power of MI7 will be upon us if we don't get to the bottom of all this," said Jeremy. "For a start, where are those two bodyguards you assigned to us?"

"Mustafa and Dontafa?" said the Sheik. "They vanished too. Right off the street, as you were chased by those devil-camels!"

Deidre gave a shudder at the memory of them, and the shudder pulled a chunky tuft out of Patsy's hair. Patsy slapped her hands to the back of her head, and spun around, glaring.

Jeremy's eyes went all shifty and his voice

went all suspicious. "Of course," he said, "whoever is controlling the robots would want to make it look like they'd vanished too."

The Sheik gulped down the last of his tea. "Perhaps you're right. I never quite trusted those two. Come, I have my helicopter on standby on the roof. The streets will not be safe."

"Hey, Patsy," said Jeremy. "Helicopters. Your favourite."

But Patsy wasn't listening. She was too busy fighting with Deidre on the carpet.

The sun beat down as the helicopter rose. The Sheik was the pilot because he liked to be the one to say all that "Roger, over and out" stuff into the radio. Jeremy was beside him, binoculars at the ready. Patsy and Deidre were on the back seat. Patsy made rude signs at Deidre, and Deidre licked Patsy's face.

"I think I'm going to be sick," growled Patsy.

The helicopter swooped over Cairo. The Sheik liked to be the one to do all that swooping stuff, too.

They could see broad, flat roofs, tiny streets, the domes of the historic mosques in the old part of the city. And it was all a sort of light brown colour. Possible puns about a Brown being in a brown place were completely ignored. Jeremy scanned the city through his binoculars.

"It's very dark down there," he said. Patsy leaned over and took the lens caps off. "Ah, but I think I'm looking at a better angle now. I can see … some people running… And over there I can see … some other people running… Mummies are after them… They're running towards each other… They've … run into each other… The mummies are still after them… They're scattering…" He put down his binoculars. "Isn't it interesting, watching the way they go in all directions like that?"

"I think they'd prefer it if we actually

helped them," said Patsy, trying to clean Deidre's dribble off her ear with a hanky.

"Quite right," said Jeremy. "We must map the robots' movements. Sheik, time to do some more of that swooping stuff, if you'd be so kind."

"Brill!" said the Sheik, and set about banking and swerving the helicopter, first in one direction, then another. Jeremy peered through his binoculars at the streets below and scribbled notes on to the back of his hand. Patsy clung to her seat for dear life. Deidre had a sneezing fit in Patsy's face.

"I really am going to be sick!" shouted Patsy, getting out her hanky again.

The helicopter swooped and dived, sometimes in order to fly over a new area of the city but mostly because the Sheik was really enjoying himself. Jeremy kept a careful count of where mummies were to be seen (at regular intervals, every two or three streets), and in which direction they were heading (the same direction, on the whole). Before long, he came to the conclusion that they'd been set out to form –

"A barrier," he said.

The MI7 book *How to Impress People,* which Jeremy had read several times, stated that now was the point at which any non-MI7 personnel present should ask an interesting question. Patsy was too busy avoiding Deidre's bad breath by pressing her hands over her face, so Sheik Yabelli stepped in and did the honours. "You mean they're protecting something?" he said.

"Precisely," said Jeremy, impressively. "They're in a roughly semicircular formation and they're moving very slowly in that direction." He pointed ahead of them. "Which means that whatever they're protecting will be in *that* direction!" He pointed behind them.

Sheik Yabelli swung the helicopter around. Directly ahead of them now, rising high above the rooftops, were three gigantic triangles.

"The pyramids," murmured Jeremy.

"The pyramids don't need protecting," said the Sheik. "They're big enough to look after themselves."

Jeremy got on with a bit of careful thinking. The helicopter flew out over the wide area of sand which separated the city from the pyramids. Deidre got ready for a really huge, nostril-cleaning sneeze.

Patsy shut her eyes tightly. "If we don't land *now,* I am *going to be sick!*"

The helicopter rapidly descended.

The group of thirty-two tourists, on a package tour organized by Sun & Sand Holidays Ltd, were at that moment enjoying a guided tour of the area which separated the city from the pyramids. They hadn't been told about the patrolling mummies. They also hadn't got over having their river cruise ruined by falling camels in Chapter Two, but the company had persuaded them not to fly home and complain to the authorities. The Sun & Sand representative was speaking to them slowly and calmly:

"So here we are, next to the magnificent pyramids, one of the ancient wonders of the world. On your left, the giant Sphinx, a human-headed statue of a lion. On your right, many charming little stalls where you can buy souvenirs and ..." (a puzzled pause) "helicopters?"

The tourists turned, curious. Sure enough, a helicopter was rapidly descending towards them. For a few moments, they looked at each other, and then they looked at the Sun & Sand rep. That delay was their big mistake.

The violent downdraft caused by the helicopter's rotors blasted sand, souvenirs and tourists in all directions. The area was engulfed in a whirlwind. Mrs Bedsit (from Hull) screamed at the top of her voice. Mr Bungalow (from Leamington Spa) was knocked unconscious by a flying souvenir stall. The Sun & Sand rep began to cry.

Patsy leapt out of the helicopter, closely followed by Jeremy, who was a bit annoyed at the way the whirlwind kept messing up his hair. Deidre, not having thumbs, was unable to undo her seat belt, and so she stayed where she was. With a cheery wave, the Sheik guided the helicopter back up into the sky, and with a quick loop-the-loop vanished into the distance.

"Which pyramid shall we try first?" said Patsy.

"We must apply careful, deductive methods to the situation," said Jeremy, combing his hair. "Let's see… Eeny, meeny, miny, mo…"

They set off for the one in the middle. The one on the right was the biggest, and therefore too obvious as a hiding place, and the one on the left was a long way away.

"It's too hot to walk," grumbled Jeremy.

Behind them, the tourists were fighting their way out from under mountains of sand and bits of shredded souvenir stall.

*   *   *

"Wow," said Patsy.

The gigantically enormous shape of the pyramid rose way up high in front of them. It was made of massive stone blocks, each the size of a wardrobe. There were a number of openings at various points up the sloping side.

"Entrances to the tombs of the pharaoh and his queen," said Jeremy. "Originally, they were sealed up, but the passageways were excavated long ago."

"Wow," said Patsy.

Shielding his eyes from the dazzling sunlight, Jeremy craned his neck to examine the entrances. Patsy kept getting a nervous tingle down her spine. It might have been leftover drops of Deidre's dribble, but it was more probably a feeling of creeping unease.

"Better get a move on," she said "Those mummies could turn up at any minute."

"There!" said Jeremy, pointing to an entrance about halfway up the pyramid.

"They're in there. All the other entrances are worn at the edges, but that one's cut nice and sharp into the stone."

"So it must be new," said Patsy.

"Right," said Jeremy. "You know, sometimes my brilliance astounds even me!"

Patsy began to clamber up the stone blocks. Jeremy tried to think of a way to ascend without having to get all hot and bothered, but he couldn't.

By the time they'd hauled themselves up level with the entrance, they were hotter and more bothered than Jeremy had dared fear. They looked back down, but that just made them feel dizzy as well. Up here, the breeze made spooky noises as it whistled around the stones, and would have pulled creepy faces too, had it been able. They stared through the entrance into the pitch-black tunnel ahead of them.

"A-a-after you," said Jeremy.

With a quick oh-for-goodness'-sake look,

Patsy marched in. Jeremy tiptoed. What neither of them knew was that it didn't matter how they proceeded. They had already been detected by an electronic early warning system, and a trapdoor was being activated.

All they could see, as they edged down the passageway, was a rectangle of sky slowly getting smaller behind them. They felt their way delicately along the smooth, cold walls. The floor was angled steeply downwards, and they could feel scatterings of sand beneath their feet.

"The robots must come in and out along here," whispered Jeremy.

"It seems pretty quiet at the moment," whispered Patsy. "Perhaps we can creep up behind them undetected."

"I reckon so," whispered Jeremy. "Looks like they've underestimated our keen intelligence and fiendish cunning."

KA-CHUNGGGG!

"WhoaaaAAAAAAAAAAaaaaaa!"

"WheeeeeaaaaEEEEEEEEEEE!"
That was the trapdoor.

Chapter 5

In which the villains are unmasked, and our heroes are done for, for sure

"Begin second stage production line!"

The voice was low, echoing around the shadowy, cavernous chamber. It came from a speaker mounted on the wall, above a line of complex-looking machines. Jeremy and Patsy were rubbing whatever bits of themselves they'd bashed on the way down the metal chute which had been lurking under the trapdoor.

"I knew I should have worn standard issue MI7 padded underpants," said Jeremy, wincing.

Suddenly, a mummy appeared out of the shadows. They froze with fear, but quickly thawed out again when they realized that it wasn't interested in doing them any damage.

It lumbered across to one of the machines, pressed a sequence of buttons, and pulled a small red lever. The machine shuddered and clunked into life, and was soon chugging away to itself, emitting the occasional hiss of steam. The mummy went on its way.

As their eyes got used to the dimness, Jeremy and Patsy could make out many such machines, arranged in rows. Between the machines trundled conveyor belts, carrying various mechanical components. In the centre of the cavern rose a series of thick pipes, feeding into a huge cone-shaped device, which was suspended above the floor, pointing down.

"It's a factory," said Jeremy. "And you don't have to be as fabulously clever as me to work out what it's making."

"How long do you reckon it'll take to make an entire robot army?" said Patsy.

"Better ask Mustafa and Dontafa," said Jeremy. "I'm convinced those so-called bodyguards are behind all this. Even the

Sheik said he didn't trust them."

"Well, now's your chance," said Patsy.

Jeremy turned in the direction Patsy was pointing. There, in a glass-sided booth marked PRISONERS, bound tightly with ropes, blindfolded and gagged, were Mustafa and Dontafa. Jeremy began to suspect that he might possibly have been wrong.

"Maybe they're bluffing," he said grumpily.

"Or maybe," said a smarmy voice behind them, "we've caught another pair of nosy parkers."

Jeremy and Patsy were surrounded by mummies. Above the mummies, standing on one of the chugging machines, were Agent Spanner and Agent Wrench. Jeremy couldn't help noticing that their smart white suits had become all wrinkled and marked in the heat of the desert.

"I told Spanner to buy more practical attire, but he wouldn't listen," slimed Agent Wrench. He sneered at the glass booth. "These two tracked down our robot camel storage depot, and now, Brown, you and your scruffy little friend can join them in the cage. It will then be lowered into a pit of fresh concrete, from which you might possibly be rescued in a thousand years or so."

"And just where are you going to get a pit of fresh concrete?" cried Patsy.

Agent Wrench wriggled a long finger, flipped a switch on the side of one of the machines and, with an electric hum, a door slid open in the floor. "Here's one I prepared earlier," he grinned, horribly. He turned to Agent Spanner. "Spanner, I'm going to check the production line. Get the mummies to deal with these two."

"Do I have to?" whined Agent Spanner. "Those mummies frighten the life out of me."

"Yes, you do!" yelled Wrench. "What kind of a criminal mastermind are you, if you can't send a few do-gooders to a nasty death! Get on with it!"

He scurried away. Agent Spanner waved in

the general direction of Jeremy and Patsy. "Umm, stick them in the concrete, mummies, if you don't mind, please," he said.

The mummies lunged, and grabbed our heroes. Jeremy and Patsy were sealed up in the glass booth, along with their bodyguards, before Jeremy could think of a single witty remark.

"We're done for, for sure," quivered Patsy.

"Err…" said Jeremy.

With a jerk, the booth was hoisted into the air. It shook violently, but it was mostly the prisoners who were doing the shaking. The oozy, grey rectangle in the floor was directly below them. The chain from which the booth was hanging was locked in position. The booth began to descend.

"I suppose shouting 'help' wouldn't do any good?" shuddered Patsy.

They soon established that bashing the glass with their fists didn't do any good either. The concrete grew nearer and nearer.

"Rock!" shouted Jeremy suddenly.

"Not yet," said Patsy, "it's still liquid."

"No! Rock the booth!" Jeremy flung all his weight against one of the glass sides. Patsy realized what he was up to and joined in. Mustafa and Dontafa were still blindfolded, so all they could do was wonder what on earth was going on. The booth swung. Jeremy and Patsy leaped at the opposite side. It swung back. The swinging motion got wider and wider until –

Sss-KRRRRRAsssSHHHHH!

– it smashed against one of the machines. The prisoners tumbled to the floor in a shower of glass.

A loudly warbling alarm sounded. Agent Spanner covered his ears. "Oh, do we have to have that awful din every time something happens?"

Agent Wrench looked up from the computer console he was working at. His face twisted into something that would have given Dracula nightmares. "Catch them!" he spat at a nearby mummy. "And keep the production line going!"

Over by the shattered booth, Jeremy and Patsy were undoing the ropes around Mustafa and Dontafa. The bodyguards flung off their blindfolds and blinked nervously as they took in their surroundings.

"Never doubted you for a minute, boys," lied Jeremy. "You try to find a way out, and alert anyone you can find. Patsy and I will fight off the mummies, shut down the factory, arrest Agent Wrench and Agent Spanner and … err … you know… On second thoughts, finding a way out is more a job for a highly trained secret agent…"

But the bodyguards had already hurried away into the darkness. Jeremy and Patsy went in the opposite direction, towards the huge, upside-down funnel-thing in the centre of the factory.

Agent Wrench checked pressure gauges and

electronic read-outs, adjusted dials and operated switches. Agent Spanner was having a nice sit-down in the corner.

The noise of the machines rose. The conveyor belts moved faster. The central funnel shook, there was a loud KA-PING and a fully-formed mummy dropped out with a crash. It stood up, its programming tuned it in to Jeremy and Patsy's location, and it moved off.

"Ha, ha, haaa, Haaa, HHaaaaaAAAAA Haaaa!" yelled Agent Wrench, among other things. He slapped his hands together with glee.

"Honestly, there's no need to get so excited," mumbled Agent Spanner.

The funnel began to tremble again. Another mummy appeared …

KA-PING! Crash!

and another …

KA-PING! Crash!

Chapter 6

In which there is a colossal explosion

....

Meanwhile, Jeremy and Patsy had quite enough mummies to contend with already. The mummies weren't nimble enough to catch them if they kept crawling underneath the conveyor belts, so they followed the line of the machines back towards the centre of the cavern.

"I thought Wrench and Spanner were MI7 agents!" said Patsy.

"They are," said Jeremy. "Or rather they were. I've got a feeling they may get the sack for this!"

"But what do they want an army of robots for?"

"Oh, come on Patsy, what would you do with an army of robots?"

"Ummm," pondered Patsy, "force the Headmaster to ban double Geography."

"Exactly," said Jeremy. "They could do whatever they want. Take over Egypt, MI7, anything. And if anyone moves against them, they just churn out more robots."

"Sounds like fun," said Patsy.

"Patsy!" cried Jeremy, shocked. "It's an appalling way to behave, and you know it! They're no better than playground bullies."

Suddenly, a bandaged arm swung out and grabbed Patsy's ankle. She twisted round and kicked with her other foot. Her boot clanged hard against the robot's ear. Its head bent inwards, sparks flew and the mechanism holding her ankle let go enough for her to pull free.

"Looks like they've learned to crawl!" said Jeremy. They rolled out from under the conveyor belt and jumped to their feet.

Agent Wrench and Agent Spanner blocked their way forward. Mummies blocked their retreat.

"Don't have to go just yet, do you?" said Agent Wrench, creepily. "We've hardly begun to make your lives a misery."

"You really are being a dreadful nuisance," added Agent Spanner.

Jeremy pulled himself up to his full height, which was about half Agent Wrench's. "You, sir, are a disgrace to the Secret Service. And so is your trained monkey here."

Agent Spanner fought back the tears. "I say we get really, really horrid with them," he quivered. "Straight away."

"Do you honestly think that disposing of us will stop you being found out?" said Jeremy. "MI7 will simply send in more agents."

Agent Wrench flung out his arms, grinning madly at the machines all around them. "By then it will be too late. Spanner's genius for electronics, and my genius for dastardly plots of international proportions, have created the ultimate weapon. Out here in Egypt, apparently on a mission, we can keep away from prying eyes while we build our factory. With the so-called curse of Psidesalad II to terrify and confuse everyone, we can test our robots in the field. We are ready for anything. Let MI7 send a hundred agents! We'll nobble the lot of them!"

"You're barmy," said Patsy.

"And you, Ginger, are history," sneered Agent Wrench. He turned to the mummies. "Attack!"

The phrase "all hell broke loose" is one which should be used carefully. In a case like this, it would imply that a lot of bangs, crunches and other destructive noises were going on. It would also imply that things were thrown, shins were kicked, and evil villains were wrestled to the ground by the best friends of secret agents. And that's exactly what did happen, so...

All hell broke loose. Jeremy dodged the fists of two advancing mummies. They ploughed into a machine, making mummy-shaped dents in it. Jeremy dashed over to Agent Wrench's computer console.

"Hold them off, Patsy, I'll try to shut down the production line!"

A gang of mummies was hanging on to various parts of Patsy, so it was more a question of them holding her off. She had Agent Wrench's collar gripped tightly in one hand and Agent Spanner's in the other, so at least they were in a tight spot, too.

"Gerrof," spluttered Agent Wrench, turning blue.

"That's not very nice, now, is it?" gasped Agent Spanner, turning purple.

Jeremy's hands fluttered over the banks of controls in front of him. He thought hard about the MI7 "Stay Cool in a Crisis" lecture he'd been to. He examined the read-outs. He checked the dials. He made a calm, rational judgment about what codes he needed to tap into the computer to shut the production line off, and pressed the ENTER key. The production line speeded up.

Mummies started dropping out of the funnel at an alarming rate. They were coming at him from all directions, homing in on the intruder. Their arms reached out.

The conveyor belt next to Patsy was whizzing along now. Agent Wrench struggled wildly.

"Too fast!" he croaked. "It'll overload!"

With a whopping great SMACK, the conveyor belt buckled and snapped. One end whipped round and slapped a line of mummies into the air. The other end did the same to Patsy. Her scream as she was hurled upwards, clutching her bottom, is unrepeatable. She landed on top of the giant funnel, slipped, and only stopped herself falling by hanging on to the thick tubes which fed into the funnel's top. Several of them were split open, and jets of steam hissed in her face.

Jeremy watched helplessly. One mummy had both his arms, and another had both his legs. Luckily, all four limbs were still attached to his body. He'd worked out where he'd gone wrong at the controls, but there was no hope of having a second go. Agent Wrench and Agent Spanner were already hurrying over to the computer console and making the adjustments needed to stop the machines overloading.

Patsy got another blast of hot steam up her nose, and pulled out her hanky as a sneeze welled up. However, she'd forgotten that her hanky was still covered in the yukky mess Deidre had coated her with during their flight in the helicopter.

"UUUrrrGGGHHggHH!" she cried, understandably.

Jeremy twisted towards her as best he could. "Patsy! Stick it in the funnel!"

Only too glad to get rid of it, Patsy stuffed the dripping hanky into one of the split tubes she was hanging on to. A sharp, blue crackle of power suddenly lit the tube from inside. She let go and dropped to the floor.

Agent Wrench and Agent Spanner stopped what they were doing. "NoOOoooo!" yelled

Agent Wrench. "You'll set the whole thing off! That slime will blow every circuit in it! My factory! My beautiful machines! My lovely world domination suit!"

The machines shook and split. One by one, in a chain reaction, they exploded.

WHUMPPPHHH!
Ka-WHhhhoOOOM!
PHHoOOWWWW!

The group of thirty-two tourists on a package tour organized by Sun & Sand Holidays Ltd were at that moment enjoying an open-air lunch by the pyramids. They hadn't got over having their tour ruined by a helicopter sandstorm in Chapter Four, but the company had persuaded them not to prosecute anyone. Their tour bus was parked nearby, ready to take them back to their hotel. The Sun & Sand representative was speaking to them slowly and calmly:

"So here we are, before we depart for rest and relaxation by the hotel pool, enjoying a traditional meal cooked specially by a team of local chefs. On your left, freshly baked loaves of bread. On your right, many dishes made to ancient recipes and ..." (a puzzled pause) "a colossal explosion?"

The tourists turned, curious. Sure enough, the top had blown off the nearest pyramid and was shooting up into the sky. A deafening series of bangs sent a gigantic ball of smoke and fire billowing into the air, and blown out ahead of it all were four figures.

The tourists watched as the figures flew in a neat arc, up, over the desert and down on top of their lunch. Jeremy and Patsy, their clothes and faces singed and smoking, crashed to an almost soft landing on the pile of bread. Agent Wrench and Agent Spanner skidded along the table, splattering food all over the tourists and into the waiting arms of Mustafa, Dontafa and the police.

Then the top of the pyramid arrived. By now, of course, it had crumbled into a couple of dozen huge, heavy blocks, and the falling blocks smashed what was left of the tourists' lunch, tour bus and nerves. Mrs Bedsit (from Hull) screamed at the top of her voice. Mr Bungalow (from Leamington Spa) was knocked unconscious by a flying lump of stone. The Sun & Sand rep wet himself.

Jeremy dusted himself down. "Another job successfully concluded, Patsy," he said proudly. "The robots around the city should have switched off too, now their control system is gone."

They wandered out across the sand, paying no attention to the wailing of the tourists, the pile of rubble surrounding the tourists or the dollops of hot food covering the tourists. Agent Wrench and Agent Spanner were already under arrest in a police car halfway to the airport.

"You know," said Jeremy, "when I write this up in my memoirs, I think I'll call the chapter How I Saved the World From Robot Domination, Single Handed."

Patsy, who'd had quite enough that day,

spent a happy few minutes burying him upside down in the sand. But there was no time for mucking about. A beeping sound was coming from Jeremy's tie…